Parineeta

Sarat Chandra Chattopadhyay

Parineeta

the Betrothed

Translated from the Bengali by

Subhransu Maitra

THORNBIRD

NIYOGI BOOKS

Published by
NIYOGI BOOKS
Block D, Building No. 77,
Okhla Industrial Area, Phase-I,
New Delhi-110 020, INDIA
Tel: 91-11-26816301, 26818960
Email: niyogibooks@gmail.com
Website: www.niyogibooksindia.com

Editor: Debika Roy Choudhry
Design: Shraboni Roy

ISBN: 978-93-86906-18-2
Publication: 2018

Printed at: Niyogi Offset Pvt. Ltd., New Delhi, India

When the *Shaktishela* struck him on the breast, Lakshman's face must have looked pretty bad and forlorn. But perhaps Gurucharan's face was looking even worse when the news arrived from within the house early in the morning itself, that his wife had just then safely borne him his fifth daughter.

Gurucharan is a bank clerk and his monthly salary is sixty rupees. Hence his thin, shrivelled frame resembles the broken, worn out horseflesh of hackney carriage, his face too wears a resigned, stoical look like them. Yet, at this dreadful good news he remained still—as if petrified—the hookah in his hand, then sat back leaning against the worn-out ancestral cushion, so shell-shocked and shattered that he couldn't even heave a sigh.

The messenger of glad tidings was his ten-year-old daughter, Annakali.

'Come on dad, let's go and see her,' she chirped.

Gurucharan looked at her face and said, 'Bring me a glass of water, dear.'

Annakali went in to fetch the glass of water. Following her exit, Gurucharan reminded himself, first and foremost, of the varied expenses that the birth of a child with its lying-in room and all the rest entailed. Next, hordes of anxious thoughts started pouring into his head like a violent torrent of third-class compartment passengers as they lunge forward like mad, clutching their luggage and trampling underfoot everybody in the way when they find the doors open as a train pulls into a station on a busy, crowded day. He remembered that this two-storey house on Bowbazar Street had been mortgaged to meet the expenses of the marriage of his second daughter last year, and six months' interest was due. Durga Puja was only a month away, he would have to buy and send *tattwa* to her family. Yesterday at the office he was unable to balance debit and credit, though he stayed back till eight in the evening and the statement of accounts must be sent to England today by twelve o' clock. Yesterday the boss issued an order which said that shabbily dressed employees would not be allowed to attend office and they would be fined. But the washerman was nowhere to be seen last week, perhaps he had disappeared with half the contents of the wardrobe of the family. Gurucharan could no longer sit leaning back; he laid himself down, lifted up the hookah and told himself, heaps of people get killed in street accidents every day in this city of Kolkata, my God, are they worse sinners than me in your eyes? Merciful God, take pity on me—make a heavy car crush me under its wheels.

Annakali arrived with a glass of water and said, 'Get up dad, here's the glass of water.'

Gurucharan rose, drank the water in one gulp, and said, 'Here dear, take the glass away.'

As she left, he lay down again.

Lalita came in and said,'Mama, here's your tea, now get up.'

Tea made him lift himself up again. As he peered into her face, he felt half his anguish melt away. He remarked,'You sat up all night without a wink of sleep, dear. Come, sit by me for a minute.'

Lalita smiled shyly and sitting down said, 'I didn't sit up all night, mama.'

No one else in the world could feel the deep invisible heartache preying on wizened, overburdened, prematurely aging Gurucharan's mind as acutely as Lalita did.

Gurucharan said,'Never mind, come—sit by me.'

As she did so, Gurucharan affectionately placed his hand on her head and suddenly exclaimed, 'If I could have married off this daughter of mine to a prince, then I would know I had pulled off a feat.'

Lalita was pouring tea without lifting her head. He went on,'You have to toil from morning till night in your poor mama's house, don't you, dear?'

Shaking her head, Lalita replied, 'Why from morning till night mama? Everybody works, so do I.'

At last Gurucharan flashed a smile. Sipping his tea he queried, 'Well Lalita, how about our lunch today?'

Lalita lifted her face and said,'Why mama, I'm going to cook it!'

Gurucharan exclaimed—'You're going to cook! Do you know how to cook, dear?'

'Yes, I do, mama. Mamima has taught me everything.'

Gurucharan put down the cup of tea and asked rather incredulously, 'Really?'

'Really. Mamima shows me how to do it—many days I cook by myself,' said Lalita, and dropped her head. Putting a hand on her head Gurucharan quietly blessed her. The news lifted his spirits and removed a serious headache.

The room he was sitting in faced the lane which went by the house. As he sat there sipping at his tea, his eyes wandered towards the window and Gurucharan called aloud, 'Hello! Is it you Shekhar out there? Come in, please, come in.'

A strapping, handsome young man stepped into the room. Gurucharan said, 'Sit down. I dare say, you must have heard about your aunt's mishap this morning.'

Shekhar replied with a gentle smile, 'What mishap? It's just that a daughter has been born?'

Gurucharan said with a sigh, 'Well—it's natural for you to say that's all, but it's only me who knows what that really means.'

Shekhar protested, 'You must not speak like that, uncle; aunty will be very hurt if she hears of it. Besides, we should gladly and joyfully receive the one whom God has sent to us.'

After a moment's pause Gurucharan resumed, 'I too, jolly well know that we should rejoice and adore her, but God isn't fair, either; he doesn't judge well, my boy. I am a poor man, why on earth should there be so many in my family? Even this house has had to be mortgaged to your father. Well, let it stay that way, I don't regret that, Shekhar. But, do look at the proof, it's right under your eyes. Here is Lalita—an orphan, a girl worth her weight in gold, she deserves to be married to a prince, no less. Tell me, how can I marry her off to any Jadu, Madhu or Hari and have no compunction about it? This daughter of mine is worth infinitely more than her weight in jewels, more than the Kohinoor kind, which shines in a king's crown. But nobody can appreciate that! I'm afraid I will have to give away such a gem because I have no money. Can you imagine the dreadful pain that life will then hold in store for me? She is thirteen now but I don't have even thirteen paisa to arrange a match for her.'

Tears brimmed in Gurucharan's eyes. Shekhar remained silent.

Gurucharan again said, 'Shekharnath, please see if you can somehow find a suitable boy for the girl among your friends. I've heard that many boys these days do not set any great store by money, it is only the bride that they inspect and select. If we can find such a boy just by chance, trust my word, Shekhar, my blessing will come true and you'll be a king. What else can I say—I live in this neighbourhood and you people take great care of us, your father indeed regards me as his younger brother.'

Shekhar nodded and said, 'Well, I'll see what I can do to help.'

Gurucharan pleaded, 'Please don't forget baba, and see what you can do. She was eight when she came here. Since then she's been living here, she's grown up and she's been studying under your tutelage. You can see—can't you—how intelligent she is, disciplined and sober, too. A slip of a girl she is—to think she'll do everything from today, cook meals and feed them—she's saddled with the whole responsibility.'

At this moment Lalita in the same instant lifted and dropped her eyes. Only a slight stretch around the corners of her lips betrayed the emotion within. Gurucharan sighed and recalled, her father had made a fortune, but he gave away every bit of it to charity leaving nothing for her when he died.

Shekhar was silent. Gurucharan went on—'And how can I say he left her nothing? All the punya that he had earned by alleviating the misery of others he bequeathed to her, otherwise how could a small girl like her have become such an Annapurna! Well Shekhar, you tell me, am I right or not?'

Shekhar broke into a smile, but said nothing in reply. When he made as if to rise and go, Gurucharan asked, 'Where are you off to so early in the day?'

Shekhar said, 'I'm going to see our barrister about a case.'

As he rose to go, Gurucharan again reminded him, 'Don't forget it, baba. She is a little dark-complexioned, but she has such a beautiful face, such a sweet smile and loving kindness that one may go to the end of the world in vain looking for her match.'

Nodding, smiling, Shekhar left. Twenty-five or twenty-six years old, he was an MA and serving his apprenticeship. He qualified as an attorney the previous year. His father Nabin Roy who had made a great fortune in the molasses trade, later quit the trade and now carried on a business of money-lending at home. His elder son Abinash was a lawyer and this Shekharnath was his younger son. His massive three-storey house towered over the neighbourhood. An open roof of this house adjoined on one side the roof of Gurucharan's house and this paved the way for great bonhomie to grow between the two families whose women used this roof route to visit one another.

Negotiations had been going on for a considerable period of time between Shekhar's family and another wealthy family residing in Shyambazar who wanted to give their daughter in marriage to him. The other day they had paid a visit to inspect the prospective bridegroom and expressed their keenness to fix an auspicious day in the coming month of Magha for the wedding. But Shekhar's mother declined to oblige and sent word through her maid that the marriage could take place only after Shekhar himself saw and selected the bride.

Nabin Roy whose only concern was money, took umbrage at what he saw as his wife's confounded response and testily remarked, 'What a thing to say! We've already seen the bride, haven't we? Let the match get finalized, and then we will go, do the *ashirvad* and inspect her properly.'

Even then his wife didn't relent and refused to give a final word to the match. That day Nabin Roy huffed, ate his lunch much later than the usual hour and took his siesta—not in the bedroom, but in the parlour.

Shekharnath was somewhat debonair in his ways. The room on the second floor in which he lived was exceedingly well-furnished. Five or six days later he could be seen standing before the large mirror in his room in the afternoon. He was busy dressing up for a visit to the family living at Shyambazar to inspect the prospective bride, when Lalita entered. She cast a glance in his direction for a moment and then asked, 'Going to see your bride, aren't you?'

Turning his eyes towards her Shekhar said, 'Here you are! Come on, help me dress so well that the bride will be quite taken with me.'

Laughing, Lalita replied, 'Afraid I'm in a hurry now Shekharda—I've come to get some money.'

She fished out a key from under the pillow and opening a drawer with the key fetched a few currency notes which she carefully counted and tucked away in a knot on the fringe of her sari and said, as if to herself, 'I keep borrowing money whenever I need to. But how can we repay it—I wonder.'

As he daintily brushed back tufts of hair, Shekhar wheeled round to face her and said, 'Don't. It is already being repaid.'

Very much at sea, Lalita just stared at him.

Shekhar said, 'You are just staring...you couldn't quite follow what I said, could you?

Lalita nodded, 'No.'

'Grow up a little more and then you will,' said Shekhar. He put on his shoes and left.

Later that night Shekhar lay silently on a couch. His mother came into the room. He sat up hastily. Ma sat down on the cot and asked, 'Well, have you been to see the girl? What does she look like?'

Shekhar beamed as he looked at his Ma's face and said, 'Fine.'

Ma's name was Bhubaneswari. Though almost fifty now, her figure was so graceful that she hardly looked older than thirty-five or thirty-six. And the mother's heart that lived inside this graceful exterior was even more young and tender. She hailed from a village and though she had been born and brought up there, she never looked out of place in the city even for a day. She retained the sweetness and the profound silence of her birthplace while taking effortlessly to the liveliness, dynamism, conduct and behaviour of the city. Even Bhubaneswari was not aware of the pride of place she held in her son's mind. Magnificent health, beauty, wealth and intelligence—Shekhar was endowed with many gifts by God but to his mind being his mother's son was God's greatest gift to him.

Ma said, 'You said "fine" and went mum!'

Shekhar smiled again and replied without looking up, 'You asked a question and I answered it.'

Ma too broke into a smile and said, 'You did, did you? How about her complexion, is she fair? Fair...say like our Lalita?'

Looking up Shekhar clarified, 'Lalita is dark, ma, she's fairer than Lalita.'

'Does she have a pretty face?'

'Not bad.'

'Then shall I ask the *karta* to finalize the match?'

Now Shekhar kept mum.

Gazing at his face for a moment or two, Ma suddenly asked, 'Well, is her education up to the mark?'

Shekhar said, 'I didn't ask them anything about it, ma.'

Really taken aback by this, Ma exclaimed, 'What do you mean… you didn't ask! You came away without enquiring about the most important thing for you people today?'

Wearing a smile on his face Shekhar replied, 'Yes ma, I forgot all about it.'

Now utterly amazed at what her son had said, she peered into his face for a moment or two. Then she broke into laughter and quipped, 'Well, I'm afraid you aren't going to marry her after all!'

Shekhar was about to say something, but kept quiet when he saw Lalita enter the room. Lalita slowly came up and stood behind Bhubaneswari who brought her round before herself using her left hand and asked, 'What is it now, darling?'

Lalita said quietly, 'Nothing ma, nothing.'

Formerly Lalita used to call her mashima, but Bhubaneswari would have none of it and told her, 'Lalita, I am not your mashima, but ma.' Lalita now called her ma. Bhubaneswari drew her closer to her breast and asked affectionately, 'Nothing really? Then did you pop in just to take a look at me?'

Lalita kept quiet.

Shekhar said, 'If she's come along to see you, when will she do the cooking?'

Ma said, 'Why should she do the cooking?'

Taken aback, Shekhar asked 'Who will do their cooking, then? Well, the other day her uncle was also saying that Lalita would do the cooking and all the rest.'

Ma laughed. Then she said, 'It doesn't matter anything to her uncle, does it? He can say what he likes. She hasn't married yet, nobody will eat her food if she cooks. I've sent along our cook—Bamunthakur, he will do the cooking. *Bada-bouma* is cooking our meal. In the afternoon, I eat my lunch at their place these days.

Shekhar saw that Ma herself had come to the rescue of this poor, miserable family. He heaved a sigh of relief and fell silent.

About a month later, one day in the evening Shekhar lay stretching on a couch in his room reading an English novel. He had quite buried himself in the book when Lalita came in and fished out the keys from under the pillow. She was now noisily unlocking a drawer in the cabinet.

Without lifting his eyes from the book Shekhar asked, 'What?'

Lalita explained, 'Taking some money.'

Shekhar grunted and continued reading. Tying up the money in a knot in the fringe of her sari Lalita stood up. She had dressed well today and she wished Shekhar to look at her person. She said, 'I've borrowed ten rupees, Shekharda.'

Shekhar said 'All right' but did not look at her. So she started fiddling with odds and ends and delayed leaving the room though there was no reason for her to stay back. But her delaying tactic failed to produce any result and slowly she left the room. But it wouldn't quite do to leave thus, she was obliged to retrace her steps and plant herself at the door.

They would go to the theatre in the evening. She knew jolly well that she could not go anywhere without Shekhar's permission. No one had ever told her anything about this, nor had it ever occurred to her to question why or seek reasons. But each living creature has its normal intelligence and her intelligence taught her that while others could do what they liked and go wherever they pleased, she could not. She was neither free, nor was the permission granted by uncle and aunt enough. Standing behind the door, she informed him quietly, 'Well, we are going to the theatre.'

Her quietly spoken words did not reach Shekhar's ears and he said nothing.

Now Lalita spoke a little louder, 'They are all waiting for me...'

This time Shekhar heard what was being said, put down the book and asked, 'What's up?'

Miffed at this Lalita retorted, 'So you did hear at long last. I said we're going to the theatre.'

Shekhar demanded, 'Who are *we*?'

'Annakali, Charubala, her uncle, and myself.'

'Who's this uncle?'

Lalita clarified,'His name is Girinbabu. Has come down here from Mungher five or six days ago. He'll be studying here for his BA degree—he is a nice man...'

'That's great—name, place of origin, occupation—I can see you've become very well acquainted with him, indeed. That's why I've seen nothing of you the last four or five days. You were busy playing cards, I guess?'

Lalita was scared by the abrupt manner in which Shekhar had suddenly started talking. She couldn't even imagine that such a question might crop up at all. She kept mum.

'Have had a high time playing cards these days?' asked Shekhar.

Lalita gulped nervously before breathing.

'It was Charu,' she said.

'Charu you say? Is that so?' As he spoke, Shekhar lifted his eyes, saw her and then said,'Well, well, you're all dressed up and ready to go. Go then.'

Lalita didn't go away and remained standing, silent and still.

Charulata was her next-door neighbour, of the same age and a pal to boot. They were Brahmo by faith. Shekhar knew all of her family except Girin. Girin had come over for a few days five or seven years ago. Till very recently he was living and studying in Bankipur. There was no need for him to visit Kolkata and he hadn't in the meantime paid any visit, either. That was why Shekhar was not familiar with him. Seeing Lalita still standing there, waiting,

Shekhar curtly said, 'What are you waiting here for? Go!' And he swiftly lifted the book to his eyes.

Having silently waited for four or five minutes, Lalita slowly asked, 'Shall I go?'

'Well, Lalita, that's exactly what I told you.'

The mood in which she found Shekhar robbed her of her keenness to go to the theatre, but she couldn't entirely avoid going, either. It had been agreed that she would pay one half of the expenses and Charu's uncle would pay the other half.

All of them were waiting impatiently for her at Charu's place and she could perfectly picture their growing impatience as she was being increasingly delayed, but she was unable to find her way out of this predicament. She did not have the nerve to go unless she was permitted to do so. So she waited another two or three minutes and then asked, 'Can I go—just for today?'

Shekhar tossed the book aside and snapped back—'Don't disturb me.'

'Lalita, go if you want to. You have grown old enough to understand what you should and should not do, what's good and what's bad for you.'

Lalita was startled. A dressing-down from Shekhar was of course old hat for her. Formerly she was used to it, but Shekhar had rarely, if at all, taken her to task like this in the last two or three years. Now, her friends were waiting, she too, was dressed to go, but disaster struck when she came up to fetch some money. What on earth could she say to them now?

Until today she was absolutely free to go and visit wherever, whoever she pleased as far as Shekhar was concerned.

She was certain of this freedom to such an extent that she had even got all dressed to go. Not only was this freedom now rudely curbed, she was also fit to die of shame as she realized for the first time in her thirteen year old life how disgraceful the reason behind this restriction really was. Her eyes brimming with tears of innocence unjustly hurt, she silently waited another five minutes and then left, wiping her eyes as she went. Once back in her room, she sent the housemaid to fetch Annakali and when the latter arrived, she handed her the ten rupees and said, 'Kali, you go to the theatre today, I am feeling very ill, please tell *sai* I can't go.'

Kali asked, 'What makes you feel ill, Sejdi?'

'I have a headache, nausea—I'm feeling very ill,' she said lying down on the bed and rolled over.

Then Charu arrived, pressing and importuning her to go; she got even aunty to intervene but could by no means persuade her to go. Now that she had got hold of the money, Annakali was raring to go. Afraid that such a flap might eventually result in the cancellation of their trip to the theatre, she drew Charu aside, showed her the money and said, Sejdi's been taken ill, she cannot go, Charudi! Look, she's given me the money, I say let's go.' Charu saw that though young, Annakali was no less quick-witted than any of them. She agreed and off they went.

Nothing was dearer than a game of cards to Charulata's mother Manorama, whose passion for cards outstripped her skills in the game. If she had Lalita as her playing partner, the partnership made up for her deficiency in skills. Lalita was a great one for cards. Since her maternal cousin Girindra's arrival, they were having massive midday card sessions in her room every day. Girin was a male and played well. So, Manorama badly needed Lalita when she was pitted against him.

It was the day after the trip to the theatre. Seeing that Lalita hadn't turned up at the appointed time, Manorama sent the maid to fetch her. Lalita was busy translating an English book into Bengali in a fat exercise book, so didn't go. When even her pal Charu failed to make her budge, Manorama herself descended on the scene, tossed away her books and declared, 'Come on, move. You won't have to play the learned judge in a court when you grow up, but play cards you must. So come away.'

Lalita found herself in an acute predicament. On the verge of tears she explained that it was impossible for her to take a break and go with her. She said she would rather go the next day. Manorama would have none of it. Finally she had a word with Lalita's mamima and whisked her away.

So that day, too, she found herself pitted against Girin in the game of cards. But it was a lackluster performance. She could not in the least bring herself to concentrate on the game. As long as it lasted, she sat rigid and stiff and got up to go even before dusk fell. Girin said, 'You sent money to buy the tickets, but didn't go yourself. I say, let's go again tomorrow.'

Nodding in disapproval Lalita said quietly, 'No, I was feeling very ill.'

Beaming, Girin replied, 'You've got over it now, come on, let's go tomorrow.'

'No, no…afraid I won't have any time tomorrow,' protested Lalita and left in a hurry. It was not only the dread of Shekhar that distracted her from cards, she was feeling ashamed of herself, too.

As at Shekhar's home, she was a regular visitor to this home too since her childhood, and mixed with everybody as if she were one of the family. Therefore, from the very beginning, she had never felt inhibited in meeting or speaking to Girindra—Charu's maternal uncle—mama. But the feeling that Girindra had grown especially fond of her as a result of the acquaintance of the last few days somehow continued to trouble her during the entire game as she sat before him. Till now she could not even imagine how embarrassing a man's fond glance could be.

Lalita popped in at her own place for a minute or two and then off she went to Shekhar's house. Hurrying into Shekhar's room she at once busied herself with work. Even as a child she had to do the odd jobs around this room; no one else would dust and put away the books and so on, tidy the table or wipe the pens and ink stands clean if she didn't. Due to her neglect, a considerable backlog had piled up and now she completely threw herself in it, sorting out the whole mess and putting everything right, before Shekhar's return.

Lalita used to hang around here whenever she had time and because she never looked on others as strangers or outsiders, nor did the people of this house consider her a stranger. When she was eight years old, she had lost her parents and arrived an orphan in her mama's family here. Since then she had been around; regarded as Shekhar's younger sister, she had been brought up and was now studying under his care.

Everyone knew that Shekhar had great affection for her, but no one knew—not even Lalita—what heights that affection had gained now. As she was always seen to have endlessly received the same kind of affection from Shekhar right from her childhood, no act on his part of giving her affection ever appears to be improper or unnatural, or no conduct on her part ever attracts notice. And precisely because it doesn't, the possibility that she might one day become a daughter-in-law of this family never occurred to anybody, neither to anyone in Lalita's family nor to Bhubaneswari.

Lalita's idea was to finish her work and leave before Shekhar's return. But she was absent-minded and didn't look at the clock. Suddenly the crunch of shoes approaching the door made her look up and she at once stepped aside.

As soon as he stepped into the room, Shekhar asked, 'Hullo, there you are! When did you get back home last night?'

Lalita didn't reply.

Shekhar slumped into a cushioned couch and reclining, asked again, 'When did you get back? Two o' clock? Three? Why are you mum?'

Lalita stood silent as before.

Annoyed, Shekhar said, 'Please go downstairs, Ma is calling you.'

Bhubaneswari sat in the kitchen getting refreshments ready. Lalita came up and asked, 'Ma, did you call me?'

'No I didn't,' she said and looking up she saw her face and asked at once, 'Why do you look so pale Lalita? Haven't had a bite yet?'

Lalita nodded her head in agreement.

Bhubaneswari said, 'Well, take the refreshments to your dada and then come back to me.'

A little later, when Lalita came upstairs with the refreshments, she saw that Shekhar still lay stretched—his eyes closed; as yet he had neither changed his clothes nor washed. Coming closer, she said, 'I've brought refreshments.'

Shekhar did not look up and said instead, 'Leave it somewhere and go.'

Holding the refreshments, Lalita stood in silence.

Without looking up, Shekhar managed to figure out that Lalita was waiting and hadn't left yet. He remained silent for a moment or two and said, 'How long are you going to wait there Lalita, I'll be late, please leave it on the table and go.'

Lalita who stood in silence was cross now and said quietly, 'Never mind if you're late, I have nothing to do downstairs, either.'

Looking into her eyes Shekhar retorted beaming, 'Now you're really talking. If you have nothing to do downstairs, may be there's something for you to do in the other house? If nothing's there, surely there's something waiting for you in the house next door? To be sure, Lalita, you have more than one house, right?'

'Sure I do,'said Lalita angrily, put down the plate of refreshments on the table with a bang and strode off.

Shekhar shouted after her, 'Please come in the evening.'

'It is too much for me—I can't keep going up and down, up and down…'said Lalita as she came away.

As soon as she came back downstairs, Ma reminded her, 'Well dear, you took the refreshments all right, but forgot the paan.'

'I'm hungry, Ma, and I'm tired too, let someone else do it, please,'Lalita said and plonked herself down.

Peering into her angry face Ma gave a chuckle and said, 'That's all right, you sit down to eat, I'll send up the maid.'

Lalita didn't say anything in reply and began to eat.

She had not gone to the theatre, yet Shekhar scolded her. So she was angry with him and did not go to see him for four or five days, but she turned up in his house around midday to do the room. Shekhar later saw his mistake and sent for her, but she refused to go.

An extremely old beggar occasionally came begging down the street in this neighbourhood. Lalita always felt a surge of pity and would give him a rupee whenever he came. She would very fondly listen to the enchanting, wonderful and impossible blessings that the beggar would reel off as he laid his hand on the money. He used to assert that Lalita had been his own mother in a previous life and he had unaccountably recognized her the moment he first saw her. And this decrepit aging son of Lalita today came calling in the morning itself and stopping at the door of her house, bellowed,'My gracious *ma-janoni,* where are you?'

Today Lalita felt rather embarrassed at being called thus. Shekhar was now in his room, how on earth could she go to his room to fetch money? Looking for help she went to her mami. But mami just had an altercation with the maid, and with a long face was now busy cooking. Sensing that she couldn't talk to her just now, Lalita came back and peeped out to find the beggar sitting pretty in the doorway, his stick leaning against the door. Lalita had never ever disappointed him and today she couldn't bring herself to turn him away empty-handed.

The beggar bellowed again.

Annakali came running and gave her the news,'Sejdi, that son of yours has come.'

Lalita implored,'Kali honey, please do me a favour. I'm tied down here, you run to Shekharda, borrow a rupee and come back to me with the money.'

Kali darted off and a little later came back running and thrusting a rupee in Lalita's hand she said,'Here, take the money.'

Lalita asked,'Did Shekharda say anything?'

'Nothing. Only asked me to take the money from his shirt pocket and I did.'

'And he said nothing else?'

'No. nothing else,' nodded Annakali and went off to play.

Lalita got rid of the beggar, but unlike other days she didn't stand waiting to hear his dazzling verbiage. She was in no mood for any stuff of that kind.

For the last few days their session of cards was going on in full swing. Today Lalita skipped the noon session—said she had a bad headache—so she slept and stayed away. Today she was really down in the dumps. In the afternoon she called Kali and asked her, 'Kali, you don't any more go to Shekharda to take lessons from him, do you?'

Nodding vigorously Kali said,'Why, of course I go.'

'Shekharda doesn't ask anything about me, does he?'

'Oh no…yes, yes, he did the day before yesterday, asked if you play cards in the noon.'

Lalita anxiously asked, 'And what did you say?'

Kali replied, 'You go to Charudidi's place to play around midday. This is what I said. Shekharda asked who are the players? I said Lalitadi, Saima, Charudidi and her mama. Okay, so who is the better player, Sejdi? Charudidi's mama or you? Saima says you play very well, right?'

Lalita did not say anything in reply but she suddenly felt very vexed and barked at Kali, 'You had no business gushing on like that, did you? You are forever poking your nose into everything, aren't you? I'm not going to give you anything from now on, I really won't.' And she left in a huff.

Kali was flabbergasted. She could not figure out the cause of this abrupt change of mood in Lalita.

The last two days went by without any game of cards being played at Manorama's place because Lalita didn't turn up.

From the moment he first saw her, Girindra had been attracted to Lalita. Manorama had suspected as much at the very outset, and her suspicion grew even firmer today.

The last couple of days saw Girin grow unaccountably eager and absent-minded. He would not go for a stroll in the afternoon, come indoors off and on and potter about the rooms. Today he came up and asked, 'Didi, we aren't going to play cards today too, are we?'

Manorama replied, 'How can we, Girin? Where are the players?' But she added at once, 'Well, no matter. There's three of us, let's play.'

Girin said without any enthusiasm, 'Three isn't enough, didi. Why not send for Lalita who lives next door?'

'She won't come.'

Gloomily Girin wondered, 'Why not? Perhaps her people asked her not to. That's it. Right?'

Manorama shook her head in disagreement and said, 'Nothing of the sort. Her uncle and aunt aren't of that type. She doesn't come of her own accord.'

Suddenly Girin perked up at this and suggested, 'In that case she will come the moment you go and ask her.' Hardly the words were out when he almost died of embarrassment.

Manorama couldn't help smiling and said, 'Well, go I must.' And a little later came back with Lalita in tow and sat down to shuffle the deck of cards.

The last two days they hadn't played, today the game of cards was going pretty well in no time. Lalita and her partner were winning. A couple of hours later Kali suddenly appeared on the scene and said, 'Sejdi, Shekharda's calling—Quick.' Lalita's face fell, drained of all colour. She stopped shuffling the cards and said, 'Shekharda hasn't gone to office, has he?'

'I don't know, he came back from office.' Kali tilted her head and left.

Lalita put down the cards, looked up at Manorama and pleaded embarrassedly, 'I am off, saima.'

Grasping her hand Manorama said, 'Why dear, let's have another game.'

Lalita at once got up and said, 'No saima, or he'll be very cross.' And hurried away.

Girin asked, 'Didi, who is this Shekharda?'

Manorama replied, 'See that big house with the gates out there?'

Girin nodded, 'Oh, that one! Does Nabin babu happen to be a relative of theirs?'

Manorama looked at her daughter, chuckled and said, 'Relative indeed! The old boy is hell-bent on grabbing any chance to get hold of even the small house of Lalita and her people.'

Girin looked amazed.

Manorama then went on to retail how Nabin Ray had lent Gurucharan money at a very high rate of interest when the latter was unable to arrange the marriage of his middle daughter for lack of funds and was obliged to mortgage his house to Nabin babu. Gurucharan was in no position to repay the loan and Nabin Ray would ultimately take over the house.

Having recounted the whole story Manorama finally remarked that the old man was very keen to pull down Gurucharan's tumbledown residence and build a big house there for his younger son Shekhar so that both the sons would each have a house of his own—which was a pretty good plan.

This bit of history saddened Girin and he asked, 'Well didi, Gurucharan babu has other daughters too, how will he marry them off?'

Manorama said, 'You are right there and then there's Lalita. She's an orphan and the poor man is her guardian. She's all grown up and must be married off within this year. In their society there's nobody who can help, caste is all they are concerned about. We are better off, aren't we, Girin?'

Girin remained silent, Manorama went on, 'The other day we got talking about it—Lalita's mami and I—she broke down and wept to me. They're at their wits' end, don't know what to do about it. Gurucharan babu is worried sick over it. I say Girin, isn't there anyone among your friends out there in Mungher who will marry a girl simply for her merits? She is a jewel of a girl.'

With a quiet melancholy smile Girin said, 'I have no such friends didi, but I think I can help them out with money.'

His father was a doctor. He had amassed a fortune and a number of properties and now everything belonged to Girin.

Manorama exclaimed, 'You will actually lend money?'

'No question of lending didi—he will pay back if he pleases, if not, he needn't.'

Manorama was nonplussed. She demanded, 'What will you gain by giving money? They are neither our kin nor do they belong to our Brahmo society and whoever lends money gratis?'

As he directed his glance at his sister's face, Girin kept smiling and replied, 'Never mind if they don't belong to our society, they are Bengali, are they not? He is absolutely broke and I have plenty of money. Please didi, why don't you go and ask him once—if he agrees, I can give the money. Lalita is neither a close relative of theirs, nor ours, so I will bear the entire cost of her marriage.'

Not that Manorama was very pleased to hear all this. Though no personal harm would be caused to her through the course of action proposed, the fact remains that many women cannot take it gladly when they see someone giving someone else so much money.

Charu was all ears and listening silently, now she jumped for joy and piped up, 'Yes mama dear, please give them the money, I'll go and tell saima straightaway.'

Her mother pulled her up, 'You keep mum, Charu. You are but a child, must not get involved in this business. I will tell them myself if there's any need to do so.'

Girin urged, 'Please do it, didi. Day before yesterday I chatted a little with Gurucharan babu over there—down the street. The way he spoke—it seems to me he is a very simple man. What do you say?'

Manorama said, 'That's exactly what I also say, and others say it too. Husband and wife are—both of them—very simple souls. That's why it's all so saddening, Girin. Perhaps he will lose the roof over his head and go on the street homeless. And you can bear witness yourself, can't you Girin? Didn't you notice how Lalita got up in a hurry and ran off the moment she was told that Shekhar babu was calling her as if her whole family were sold out to them. And though they may try hard to keep Nabin Ray sweet and pleased, nobody expects they will be able to get out of his clutches.'

Girin persisted, 'So you'll go and ask them didi, won't you?'

'Well, yes, I will. So much the better if you offer money and come to their rescue.' Then at once she flashed a little smile and quipped, 'Now really, Girin, why are you so keen on it?'

'Not exactly keen didi, it is just that we must help each other to tide over difficulties.' Having said that he withdrew—his face betraying a little shyness. However, hardly had he stepped out of the room when he turned and coming back in, he sat down again.

His didi asked, 'Why, you're back again!'

Smiling, Girin explained, 'You were so full of moans, didi. But all this may not be true, after all.'

Taken aback, Manorama asked, 'Why?'

Girin went on, 'A poor girl does not throw around money the way Lalita does, you know. The other day we went to the theatre, she did not go herself, yet she sent ten rupees through her sister. Why not ask Charu, she throws around a lot of money. Indeed, you see she spends no less than twenty to twenty-five rupees every month to meet her own expenses.'

Manorama remained incredulous.

Charu said, 'It's true, ma. That is Shekharda's money. It's nothing new; she opens Shekharda's almirah and takes money and she's been doing it ever since she was a child. And nobody minds it, either.'

Manorama looked at her daughter and demanded rather incredulously, 'Does Shekhar babu know that Lalita takes money from the almirah?'

Nodding affirmatively Charu replied, 'He does. She goes and opens the almirah with the key and comes away with money even when he is present. Who do you think gave so much money last month for Annakali's dolls' house wedding? It was Lalita sai who gave all the money.'

After a moment's reflection Manorama observed, 'Well, I would not really know. But it's also true that the old man's sons aren't hard-hearted skin-flints like their father, they've inherited their mother's nature, and hence they are caring and kind. Besides, they say Lalita is a very good girl, she has been around here since her childhood, she calls them dada, that's why they are very kind and generous to her. Hello, Charu, you often go there—tell me, is Shekhar going to get married in the coming month of Magha? I've heard the old man will make a lot of money out of the marriage.'

Charu said, 'Yes ma, he is going to get married this very Magha and everything's been arranged.'

Gurucharan is the kind of man whom anyone irrespective of age can engage in a conversation. After three or four days of casual conversation, his acquaintance with Girin developed into a permanent friendship. Because Gurucharan lacked any firmness of mind or character, he never expressed the least resentment even if he was beaten in an argument though he was very fond of debates.

He'd extended a standing invitation to Girin to have tea at his place in the evening. Usually he returned home from office in the evening and immediately after the wash he would ask, 'Lalita dear, is tea coming? Kali go, go and fetch your Girin mama.' Then they had their tea and got on with their discussions.

Occasionally sitting behind her mama Lalita would listen to their arguments. On such occasions Girin would wax spectacularly eloquent and argumentative. Oftener than not their debate centered on criticism of the ways of modern society—its heartlessness, indefensible high-handedness and persecution and all this was only too true.

On the one hand all this was utterly indefensible, on the other everything Girin said unerringly struck chords in Gurucharan's bruised, anguished mind. Finally he would shake his head and concur, 'That's right, Girin. Everybody wants to marry off their daughters to boys of good families at the proper time, but how can we? Society says, go ahead—get your daughters married, they are old enough for marriage. But the blessed society itself can't step forward and arrange the marriage. You're on the button there, Girin. Why, consider my case, even this house has been mortgaged and the day isn't far off when I with my family will go on the street homeless. Society will not then say, come, we'll take you in, will it, eh?'

Girin would perhaps keep quiet and Gurucharan would himself go on, 'Only too true. It's better to lose your caste than remain in such a society. Perhaps I'd starve, but I would at least live in peace. A society that doesn't understand the misery of the miserable, doesn't give you courage in times of danger but only bullies you and jumps down your throat—this society isn't mine or of the poor like me. It's for the rich. So much the better, let them come in, out we go,' he would say and then abruptly go silent.

It was not only that Lalita listened attentively to the reasons and arguments advanced, at night in bed she went over them weighing them in her mind till she fell asleep. Each word spoken was being deeply etched in her mind. She would tell herself, Girin babu's arguments are really eminently justified.

She was very fond of her mama Gurucharan and whatever Girin said in his defense acquired the aura of infallible truth in her eyes. Her mama is sick with worry on her account, he even neglects to eat properly—her poor mama who has no enemies in the world has had to endure all this hardship only because he took her in. But why?

Why on earth should mama lose his caste? But he wouldn't lose caste if I got married now and became a widow soon afterwards and came back to him. Yet what difference does it make? She would recall these arguments of Girin with a heavy heart and go through them with a fine-tooth comb even as sleep came over her.

Lalita could not but concur with and revere whoever sensed her mama's misery and spoke up for him. She began to sincerely respect Girin. Gradually like Gurucharan she too would look forward to tea-time in the evening.

Formerly Girin used to address Lalita as '*aapni*'. Gurucharan didn't approve of it and said, 'Why call her aapni, Girin, call her '*tumi*' instead. Since then he addressed her as tumi.

One day Girin asked her, 'You don't drink tea Lalita, do you?'

Without lifting her head Lalita shook her head and Gurucharan said, 'Her Shekharda has forbidden it. He does not approve of women drinking tea.'

Lalita managed to guess that Girin was none too pleased to hear the reason.

The day was Saturday. The evening session lasted longer than on other days. Tea was over, Gurucharan was not at his enthusiastic best in the conversation today and at times he somehow grew absent-minded.

Girin could easily see this and enquired, 'Are you perhaps feeling rather tired and out of sorts today?'

Putting away the hookah Gurucharan said, 'Why, I am physically quite well.'

With some hesitation Girin asked, 'Anything gone wrong at the office…'

'No, nothing of that sort, either,' said Gurucharan and stared at Girin rather taken aback. Utterly simple-minded as he was, Gurucharan could not at all perceive that his conduct had betrayed the anxiety inside him.

Formerly Lalita used to remain absolutely quiet, but of late she was chipping in with an occasional remark. She said, 'Yes mama, perhaps there is something weighing on your mind.'

Gurucharan laughed and remarked, 'Oh, that's it. Yes dear, you've guessed it right, I am in a rather disturbed frame of mind today.'

Both Lalita and Girin continued to look at his face.

Gurucharan explained, 'Nabin-da knows everything, yet he said some really cutting things to me as we stood in the street talking. But I cannot really blame him either, six months have gone by and I haven't been able to pay even a paisa by way of interest, let alone the principal.'

Quickly sensing the direction towards which the conversation was moving, Lalita was at once anxious to keep the whole business under wraps lest her mama who was not in the least pragmatic should let on to Girin revealing embarrassing matters of the family. In consternation she swiftly chimed in, 'You needn't worry mama, those things will be sorted out later.'

But Gurucharan refused to take the escape route opened by her. Instead he smiled gloomily saying, 'What will be sorted out later, dear? Girin, the fact of the matter is that this little mother of mine wants that her aging son should be free from all worries. But Lalita, people outside are not at all willing to pay any attention to your mama's woes.'

Girin asked, 'What did Nabin babu say today?'

Lalita did not know that Girin was familiar with the whole story. She was very indignant at what she considered to be improper prying curiosity on his part.

Gurucharan made a clean breast of it. Nabin Ray's wife had since long been suffering from dyspepsia. Due to a recent deterioration of the ailment doctors advised a change of air for her. Money was needed. Therefore, Gurucharan would have to clear all the interest due as well as repay some part of the principal.

For a moment or two Girin remained still, then said quietly, 'I have been wanting to tell you something, but haven't been able to say it till now. If you do not mind, I want to tell it today.'

Gurucharan broke into laughter and replied, 'Nobody ever hesitates to speak to me about anything under the sun, Girin, so, what's it?'

Girin said, 'I've heard didi say that Nabin babu lends money at a very high rate of interest. So this is what I have to say—a great deal of my money is lying idle. I have no use for it. But he needs money. Then why not pay back the loan?'

Both Gurucharan and Lalita were astonished and stared at him. With great hesitation Girin went on, 'Since I have no pressing need for money right now, you may return it when it is convenient for you. They need the money, that's why I am saying…'

Slowly Gurucharan asked, 'Will you give the entire amount?'

Without looking up Girin replied, 'Well, that's no problem if it helps them…'

Gurucharan was about to say something in reply when Annakali came running in. 'Sejdi quick, quick, Shekharda is asking you to get dressed—we're going to the theatre,' she said and dashed off in exactly the same way as she had darted in.

Seeing her eagerness Gurucharan couldn't help laughing. Lalita remained still.

A moment later Annakali returned and exclaimed, 'Why Sejdi, you're still sitting here but we are all waiting for you.'

Even then Lalita did not display any willingness to rise. She was keen to know how the conversation would conclude. But Gurucharan glanced smilingly at Kali's face, patted Lalita on the head and said, 'Well ma, you had better go now, don't be late. Apparently they are all waiting for you.'

Hence Lalita had to get up and go. But before she left, she cast a glance of profound gratitude at Girin and slowly departed and Girindra noticed it.

About ten minutes later Lalita, all dressed up and ready to go, once again silently came back into the parlour on the pretext of bringing paan for Gurucharan.

Girin was gone. Gurucharan was alone and lay back—his hand resting on the plump pillow, tears streaming down from his closed eyes. Lalita perceived that these were tears of joy. Precisely for this reason she did not interrupt his meditation and left as silently as she had arrived.

A little later when she arrived in Shekhar's room, her eyes were brimming over with tears. Kali was not there, she was the first to have got into the carriage. There was only Shekhar in the room who stood quietly, perhaps waiting for Lalita herself. He looked up and noticed her tearful eyes.

He was very vexed because he had seen nothing of her in the last ten days. But now forgetting his vexation he asked anxiously, 'Hullo, are you crying?'

Lalita bent her head, nodding vigorously.

Her total absence during the last few days had brought about a change in Shekhar's mind; so he came closer and suddenly lifted up Lalita's face with his hands and exclaimed, 'Why, you're really crying, what's the matter?'

Unable to restrain herself any longer, Lalita slumped down and hiding her face in the fringe of her sari she broke down and sobbed.

Nabin Ray received to the last paisa all the interest due and the principal and then gave back the deed of mortgage and asked, 'I say Gurucharan, who gave you the money?'

Humbly Gurucharan replied, 'Please, do not ask anything about that, dada, I am forbidden to say anything.'

Nabin was not at all pleased to get back the money; he neither expected it, nor did he wish it to happen. On the other hand, he had up his sleeves his own plan to pull down Gurucharan's house and build a new mansion in its place. Full of sarcasm he retorted, 'Well, it is forbidden to say anything and no wonder that, *Bhaya*, the fault is not yours, but mine. Surely it is a fault to want to get the money back; they are right when they say that the Kaliyuga has arrived.'

Stung to the quick, Gurucharan protested, 'You mustn't say that, dada. I managed to pay back the debt of your money, but I am unable to pay back the debt of kindness I owe you.'

Nabin laughed. He was a hardboiled man. If he were in the habit of trusting words of the kind spoken by Gurucharan, he would not be the rich man that he had become by carrying on the trade of selling molasses. He said,'If you had such thoughts at the back of your mind, bhaya, you wouldn't pay back the money like this. True, I asked for the money, but I asked because your *bouthan* is ill. Not for any other personal necessity. Well, what kind of interest did you pay when you mortgaged the house?'

Gurucharan shook his head in disagreement, 'I didn't mortgage the house—there was no talk of interest, either.'

Incredulous, Nabin countered,'Really,without any interest?'

'Yes dada, it is really like that. The boy is exceedingly honest, kind too.'

'Boy? Who's this boy?'

Gurucharan did not say anything in reply and remained quiet. He shouldn't really have let on like that.

Nabin could guess his feelings. He laughed quietly and said,'Since you're forbidden, you had better not say anything. Nevertheless, I have seen a great many things in my life and let me warn you bhaya, whoever your benefactor is, beware that he doesn't get you in trouble though he has helped you a lot.'

Gurucharan did not say anything in reply, offered namaskar and came back home clutching the deed of mortgage.

About this time of the year Bhubaneswari would go up country almost every year to spend some days out there. She had chronic dyspepsia and such a trip helped improve the state of her health.

Not that it was a severe ailment. Nabin had exaggerated things in his effort to induce Gurucharan to cough up the money. Nevertheless, preparations were being made for the trip.

On that day Shekhar was busy packing the fancy things he considered indispensable into a leather suitcase.

Annakali came in and asked, 'You're going tomorrow, aren't you?'

Looking up from the suitcase Shekhar addressed her, 'Kali, please call your Sejdi, it's high time she packed up things.'

Lalita accompanied Bhubaneswari on her trips every year.

Shekhar was expecting that this year too, she would go.

Shaking her head Kali said, 'This time Sejdi isn't going.'

'Why not?'

Kali said, 'Fancy her going! How can she? She will get married in the month of Magha or Phalguna, baba is busy looking for a suitable boy.'

Speechless, Shekhar stared without batting an eyelid.

Whatever she had picked up on the domestic grapevine, Kali now regurgitated enthusiastically in a whisper, 'Girin babu has said money is no problem, we need a good bridegroom. Baba won't go to office today either, after lunch he'll go to inspect a boy. Girin babu will also go with him.'

Quiet and still, Shekhar went on listening and seemed to understand—at least partly—why Lalita was not any more willing to come.

Kali went on, 'Girin babu is a very nice man, Shekharda. Baba had mortgaged our house to Nabin uncle—you know and baba was saying that after a couple of months all of us would have to go on the street begging. So Girin babu gave the money. Yesterday baba went and paid back all the money to uncle. Sejdi was saying we have nothing else to be afraid of. Isn't it true, Shekharda?'

Shekhar could say nothing in reply and continued to gaze as before.

Kali asked, 'What are you thinking of, Shekharda?'

At this Shekhar seemed to wake up as if from a trance and quietly replied, 'Nothing, dear Kali. Now please hurry up, go and call your Sejdi, tell her I'm calling. Now run.'

Shekhar remained seated and glanced at the open suitcase. The things he'd need for the journey and the ones he could do without became indistinguishable and merged into one another before his eyes.

Responding to his summons Lalita came upstairs and at first saw through an opening in the window that her Shekharda was sitting on the floor and gazing fixedly at it. His face wore an expression she had never seen before. She was both surprised and scared. As she slowly drew closer and stood before him, Shekhar said 'Come,' and quickly rose to his feet.

Lalita quietly asked, 'Did you call me?'

'Yes,' said Shekhar and after a pause he resumed, 'Ma and I are going up country and we are taking the morning train tomorrow.

I don't think we'll return very soon. Here, take the keys. In the drawer over there you will find money for your expenses.'

Lalita always accompanied them on such trips. The moment her eyes fell on the open suitcase, she vividly recalled how gladly she had packed up all the things needed for the last journey. Now Shekhar was doing it all by himself.

Turning his face away from her direction, Shekhar coughed to clear his throat and said, 'Take care, and if you need anything urgently, collect my address from Dada and write me a letter.'

Then both of them fell silent. Lalita now winced with a sense of shame when she reflected that Shekhar was aware that she wasn't going with them this time and perhaps he also knew why.

Abruptly Shekhar said, 'Well, you may go now, I'll pack up these things. Time's getting on, I must go to the office, too.'

Lalita kneeled down before the suitcase and said, 'You go and have your bath, I'll do the packing for you.'

'Ah, that's better,' said Shekhar, dropped the bunch of keys before Lalita and as he stepped out of the room, he suddenly stopped and asked, 'Surely you haven't forgotten the things I usually need?'

Her head bent, Lalita was examining the contents of the suitcase and did not say anything in reply.

Shekhar went downstairs and after questioning his mother found that everything that Kali had told him was true. It was also true that Gurucharan had paid back the loan. It was also a fact that vigorous efforts were being made to find a bridegroom for Lalita. Without asking any more questions he went off to shower himself.

A couple of hours later when he went back to his room after lunch to get dressed for office, he was really in for a surprise.

All this while Lalita had done nothing but sat still resting her head on the lid of the suitcase. She started at the noise made by Shekhar's approaching footsteps, lifted her face for a moment and then bent her head again. Her eyes were the colour of crimson *jaba* flowers.

But Shekhar hardly noticed it. As he was getting dressed to go to office, he casually remarked, 'You won't be able to do it now, Lalita. Come back later and do it.' Then he left. He had made no mistake in guessing the cause of her reddened eyes but would not dare to say anything till he thoroughly weighed every aspect of the whole thing in his mind.

When Lalita took tea to her mama in the parlour in the afternoon, she suddenly shrank in embarrassment. Shekhar was sitting there. He had come to say goodbye to Gurucharan before his departure the next day.

Her head bent, Lalita prepared two cups of tea which she put before Gurucharan and Girin. Girin at once asked, 'Why don't you offer Shekhar babu a cup of tea, Lalita?'

Without lifting her face Lalita replied, 'Shekharda doesn't drink tea.' Girin didn't say anything in reply; he was reminded of Lalita's own example. Shekhar did not drink tea himself and did not want others to drink tea either.

Picking up the cup of tea, Gurucharan began to talk about the bridegroom. 'The boy is doing his BA,' he said and praised him a great deal and concluded, 'yet our Girin isn't pleased. Of course the boy isn't much to look at, certainly not very handsome, but a male has hardly any use for good looks. It's enough if he has merit.'

It appeared that Gurucharan would heave a sigh of relief only when the marriage took place.

Shekhar had just made Girin's acquaintance. He cast a glance in Girin's direction and said chuckling, 'Why isn't Girin babu pleased? The boy's studying and he is well off—indeed a good bridegroom.'

Though he asked the question, Shekhar exactly knew why Girin was not pleased with the bridegroom and would never be in future either. But Girin could not at once answer the question and blushed a little. Shekhar noticed this too, rose and said, 'Kaka, I am taking Ma up country and we are leaving tomorrow. Please don't forget to inform us in good time.'

Gurucharan remonstrated, 'Of course baba, you are my own people. Besides, nothing can be done if Lalita's Ma is not present. What do you say, Lalita?' laughing he turned his head and asked, 'well-when did she leave?'

Shekhar said, 'She fled the moment we started talking about marriage.'

Gurucharan suddenly grew grave and observed, no wonder she ran away. After all, she has become tactful and sensible, too. Then he sighed and said, 'My daughter is Laxmi and Saraswati rolled into one! Shekharnath, such a girl is indeed the blessing of rare good fortune.'

As he spoke these words, such an ineffable and sweet expression of profound affection filled his emaciated, thin countenance that both Girin and Shekhar could not help bowing to him in deep respect in their heart.

Lalita had quietly fled from the tea party and stolen into Shekhar's room. Under a bright gas light she lugged out a suitcase and got busy folding and packing Shekhar's warm clothes into it. When she saw Shekhar come in, she lifted her head, glanced at his face and remained speechless, astonished, and frightened.

Lalita had difficulty recognizing Shekhar who had changed and altered inside one hour as utterly as the man who emerges from a law court devastatingly altered, having lost everything in a court battle. His countenance bore the look of someone who had lost all his possessions in the world.

In a choked voice he asked, 'What are you doing, Lalita?'

Instead of answering the question Lalita drew closer, grasped Shekhar's hand with both her hands and asked in a tearful voice, 'What's happened, Shekharda?' She was about to cry.

'Why…nothing,' said Shekhar forcing himself to smile. At the touch of Lalita's hand his face seemed to partly recover its loveliness. He sat down on the cot close at hand and asked in turn, 'What are you up to?'

Lalita said, 'I forgot the heavy overcoat and came up to put it in the suitcase.'

Shekhar chose to listen. Having somewhat pulled herself together by then, Lalita went on, 'The last time we went, you were very uncomfortable on the train because though you had quite a few long coats none was very warm. So the first thing I did after our return was that I gave your measurements and placed an order with the tailor for this.' So saying, she brought the heavy overcoat over for Shekhar to see.

Shekhar sat fingering the coat and said, 'But you told me nothing about it?'

Lalita smiled and retorted, 'You're a dandy. If I did, you'd not let me order such a heavy coat, would you? That's why I didn't tell you, but I had it made and ready for use.' She took away the coat, put it back in place and added, 'You see, it's here, right on top of everything, just open the suitcase to find it. Don't forget to put it on if it's cold out there.'

'Yes,' said Shekhar. He stared with unblinking eyes for a while, and then abruptly said, 'No, it can never be.'

'Can never be what? You won't put it on?'

Shekhar quickly clarified, 'No, it's not that…it's a different thing. Well Lalita, do you know if Ma's things are packed and ready?'

Lalita replied, 'Yes, I do. I packed her things myself a couple of hours ago.' Once again she carefully examined the contents of the suitcase and began to fasten the lock.

For a few seconds Shekhar was silent, then glanced at her and asked, 'Well Lalita, can you tell me how I'll manage and get by next year?'

Her eyes lifted, Lalita wondered, 'Oh...why?'

'Bhai, I only can see jolly well why,' said Shekhar and hardly had the words been out when in an effort to deflect attention from what was said, he feigned cheerfulness and started gushing, 'But before you get married, please do let me know where you keep my things—otherwise I won't be able to find them when I need them most.'

Lalita got cross and said, 'Shut up...'

Shekhar finally laughed and said, 'Shut up is fine, but what is to be done really? I'm fond of a thousand things but don't have an ounce of housekeeping skills. A servant can't be expected to do all these things, either. Well, I think I will have to follow your mama's example, cut down necessities to the essential needs and use only one set of clothes come what may.'

Lalita flung down the bunch of keys on the floor and ran away.

Shekhar yelled after her, 'Please do come once tomorrow morning.'

Lalita pretended not to hear and tore down the stairs to arrive on the first floor. When she got home, she saw that Annakali was busy threading a garland of marigolds in a corner of the moonlit roof. Lalita sat down by her and asked, 'Kali, what are you doing out here in the cold?'

Without looking up Kali replied, 'Making a garland. You see, my daughter is getting married tonight.'

'But you didn't tell me, did you?'

'It's been arranged in a hurry, Sejdi. Baba glanced through the *panjika* and said there's no other auspicious day in this month save today. Daughter's grown up and must be married off, so I've had to arrange somehow. Please give me two rupees, Sejdi. I'll send somebody to buy refreshments.'

All smiles, Lalita said, 'When it comes to money, you look to Sejdi. There's some money on the bed under my pillow. Go and get it. And Kali, is marigold fit for a marriage?'

Kali replied seriously, 'It is fit enough. If there's no other flower, it'll do. Sejdi, I married off quite a few daughters, I know everything.'

Then she went downstairs to arrange for refreshments. Lalita sat down in Kali's place to make garlands.

A little later Kali came back and reported, 'Everybody has been informed except Shekharda. I must now go and tell him, or he will be offended.' She left for Shekhar's house.

Kali was a seasoned housekeeper and did everything methodically. Having informed Shekharda she came down and said, 'Shekharda needs a garland, Sejdi. Please go and give him the garland and come back quick.'

'Meanwhile I'll get on with the arrangements—the *lagna* has set in, there's no time now.'

Lalita shook her head and said, 'I can't go Kali, you go and give him the garland.'

'Well, go I must. Give me the large one,' she said, holding out her hand.

Lalita was about to hand over the garland, but on second thoughts she said, 'No, I think I'll go and give him the garland.'

Kali said on a serious note, 'Yes, you had better, Sejdi. I have so many things to do, I don't get a breather to die even.'

Her expression and the way she said all this made Lalita chuckle. 'Quite a granny—aren't you?' said Lalia and went off to see Shekhar. Standing near the threshold she could see that Shekhar was busy writing a letter. She opened the door, stole up and stood behind him; even then Shekhar wasn't aware of it. She paused for a moment, then intending to startle Shekhar out of his wits she dexterously put the garland over his head round his neck and swiftly ducked by the cot.

Startled, Shekhar at first said, 'Hullo Kali!' But the very next moment craning his neck he spotted Lalita ducking, at once grew very grave and exclaimed, 'Oh, what have you done Lalita!'

Lalita rose to her feet and rather frightened by Shekhar's grave mien she now asked, 'What's wrong?'

Without relaxing his gravity in the slightest degree Shekhar countered, 'Why, don't you know? Go and ask Kali what happens on such a night if you put a garland around somebody's neck?'

Now the penny dropped. In a flash she went crimson in the face from enormous embarrassment and repeatedly mumbling to herself, 'Oh no…never…', she ran out of the room.

Shekhar called after her, 'Lalita don't go, come back—listen. It's important…'

Shekhar's call caught her ears all right but she was hardly in a state of mind to listen. Unable to halt anywhere she ran till she came into her room, at once closed her eyes and lay down on the bed.

For the last five or six years she had grown up in close proximity to Shekhar, but till now she had never heard him speak as he did a moment ago. On the other hand Shekhar who was phlegmatic, never made fun of her and even if he ever did, she could never imagine him mouthing such a shameful jest.

Wincing with shame she kept lying down for fifteen or twenty minutes, then sat up. Still, she was scared of Shekhar and since he said he had got something important for her to do, she sat thinking whether she should go or not. And now the voice of the man who worked in Shekhar's house rang out—

'Lalita-di where are you? Chotobabu is calling you.'

Lalita stepped out and quietly said, 'You go, I'm coming.'

She went up, pushed the door ajar and saw that Shekhar was still busy writing letters. She remained silent for a while, then slowly asked, 'What's it?'

Still writing Shekhar said, 'Come closer, I'll tell you.'

'No, tell me from where you are.'

Shekhar laughed in his mind and quipped, 'You did this strange thing all of a sudden, didn't you?'

Lalita angrily barked, 'Now you're at it again!'

Now facing her Shekhar said, 'I'm not to blame! You did it yourself.'

'I did nothing. Please give it back to me.'

Shekhar explained, 'That's exactly why I sent for you. Come closer and I'll give it back to you. You did one half of it…come closer, let me do the rest and complete it.'

Lalita fell silent behind the door and after a pause said, 'I am telling you frankly, if you go on cutting jokes of this kind, I'll never come before you again—I say, let's have it back…'

Turning to the table Shekhar picked up the garland and said, 'Come and take it.'

'You toss it to me.' Shaking his head Shekhar declared, 'You're not going to get it unless you come closer.'

'Well, I won't have anything to do with it then,' said Lalita indignantly and left.

Shekhar shouted after her, 'But the thing's only half done—.'

'So be it,' retorted Lalita angrily who was now really angry and off she went.

Though she came away, she didn't go downstairs. Strolling across the east-facing roof she stood quietly holding the railing. The moon was in the sky overhead and the world was awash with the wan moonlight of winter. And high above was the transparent clear blue sky. Once she cast a glance in the direction of Shekhar's room, then looked up and away. Now her eyes smarted and filled with tears of shame and resentment.

Not that she was too young to fully understand the drift of those words, then why subject her to such heartless jokes! She was old enough to realize how insignificant, how lowly she was. She knows fully well that because she was a helpless orphan everybody gave her affection and cared for her—Shekhar and his Ma did, too. There was nobody she could call her own. And since no one was really responsible for her, Girindra—though in no way related to her—could bring up the subject of coming to her rescue.

Closing her eyes she told herself: in the city of Kolkata her maternal uncle's position was way below that of Shekhar and his family and she in turn was dependent on her mama as well as a burden for him. On the other hand, negotiations were on for Shekhar's marriage to a suitable bride from an equally affluent family. Sooner or later Shekhar would marry into such a family. She had also heard Shekhar's Ma talk about what a fortune Nabin Roy would make by way of dowry out of this marriage.

Then what made Shekhar humiliate her today in this way! Absorbed in those thoughts Lalita was thinking hard and gazing vacantly ahead of her when she started and turning her head found Shekhar smilng silently. And the marigold garland which she had a little while ago put around Shekhar's neck had come back to her the same way and now lay coiled around her neck. In a voice almost distorted and choking with sobs, she managed to get the words out—'Why did you do it?'

'Why did you yourself do it?'

'I did nothing,' she said and at once reached for the garland with one hand to tear it up but stopped midway as she suddenly looked into Shekhar's eyes.

The courage to tear up the garland drained away from her but she broke into sobs and said, 'You're insulting me like this because I have no kin or people of my own!'

Until now Shekhar was silently smiling, but now he was taken aback by the way she talked. Certainly this was not a childish outburst. He exclaimed, 'I insulted you! No. It's you who are insulting me.'

Rather scared now, Lalita wiped her eyes and asked timidly, 'How did I insult you?'

Shekhar remained still, then added in a normal tone, 'Just give it a little thought and you'll at once see how. These days you've been going too far Lalita, I have just put a stop to it before leaving for abroad.' He fell silent.

Lalita didn't talk back and stood still without looking up. Both of them remained silent under the bright moonlit sky. Only the sound of the conch being blown repeatedly could be heard to celebrate the wedding of Kali's dolls.

A little later Shekhar said, 'You'd better not stand out here in the cold, go downstairs.'

'I'm off,' said Lalita and bent down to touch Shekhar's feet with her forehead in a gesture of pranam. Then she rose to her feet and slowly asked him, 'Before you go, please tell me what I should do.'

Shekhar laughed, hesitated once, then he took her in his arms, drew her closer towards himself and bending his head locked his lips with hers and said, 'I don't have to tell you anything, you yourself will get to understand things beginning today.'

A romantic thrill ran down her body from head to foot and she trembled.

She drew back and asked, 'Did you do what you did because I somehow managed to make you wear the garland?'

Grinning Shekhar shook his head and explained, 'No, in fact I have been thinking it over for a very long time but I wasn't able to come to a decision till now. Today, I have come to a decision, because it's only today that I realized I cannot live without you.'

Lalita said, 'But your father will be furious when he gets wind of it and Ma will be sad if she gets to hear of it…no it can't be Shekharda…'

'True, Baba will be angry, but Ma will be very happy indeed. Be that as it may, what was fated to happen has happened. Neither can you reverse it, nor can I. Well, go down and offer pranam to Ma.'

About three months later, Gurucharan with a gloomy face stepped into Nabin Roy's parlour one day and was about to sit down on the carpet, when the latter yelled his disapproval, 'No no no, not here, go and sit on that cot over there. I can't go and have a bath at this unearthly hour. Well, have you really lost your caste?'

Gurucharan sat down on the cot at the far end with his head bent.

Four days ago he had been duly initiated and become a Brahmo. This news—hyped up, blown sky-high and variegated—reached the ears of Nabin who was a conservative Hindu. Nabin peered across with glowering eyes and sparks seemed to fly from them. But Gurucharan sat quiet and silent—head bent as before.

There was no end of the moaning and crying in his house ever since he went and converted without consulting anyone.

Nabin bellowed again, 'Well come on, tell me, is it true or not?

Lifting his tearful eyes Gurucharan admitted, 'Yes, it is true.'

'Why did you do it? Your salary is sixty rupees only and you—.' Nabin Roy was so angry that words failed him.

Gurucharan wiped his eyes, cleared his choked voice and said, 'I was out of my mind, dada. I was so miserable I couldn't decide whether to go and hang myself or become a Brahmo. At last I decided it was better to become a Brahmo than commit suicide and I converted.'

Wiping his eyes Gurucharan shuffled off.

Nabin bawled after him—'Nice thing you've done. You couldn't hang yourself, so you went and strung up the whole caste instead. Get lost. Don't you ever dare show us your evil face this side of the street. You'd better keep the company of those who have become your counselors now—marry off your daughters to low-caste chaps,' he said turning his face away.

At first in a fit of fury and resentment Nabin was at a loss to decide what he'd do. Gurucharan had slipped out of his clutches and there was hardly any chance of his slipping back in. Hence, thrashing about in futile fury and unable to find an immediate means of besetting and troubling Gurucharan, he hit upon an expedient, engaged a mason that very day and had a huge wall built across the roof blocking the way from one house to the other.

In a distant province far away from home, when Bhuvaneswari heard of it from Shekhar, she couldn't help crying and said, 'Shekhar, who do you think advised Gurucharan to do it?'

Shekhar surely surmised who had advised Gurucharan to convert. But instead of mentioning it he argued, 'But Ma, you people would have anyway ostracized him one of these days. I can't imagine how he could have managed to marry off so many daughters.'

Shaking her head in disagreement Bhuvaneswari observed, 'Nothing gets held up forever, Shekhar. And if one has to give up their caste in advance for this reason, heaps of people will have to do it. God would have taken care of those he has sent to this world.'

Shekhar kept quiet. Bhuvaneswari wiped her eyes and resumed, 'If I had brought Lalita out here with me, I would have had to find a way out and I would have done that. I didn't know that Gurucharan didn't let her come because he had such plans up his sleeve. I thought they were trying to arrange her marriage.'

A little embarrassed, Shekhar glanced at her and said, 'Well Ma, why not do it after you return home? Not that she has become a Brahmo herself—it was her uncle who converted. Nor is he her closest kin. Lalita is living with them because she has none she can call her own.'

Bhuvaneswari thought it over and replied, 'That's right. But the kind of man your father is, he'll never agree to it. Perhaps he won't let us go and see them any more.'

Shekhar had had more than his fair share of this apprehension; he said no more and left.

After this he lost all his zest for prolonging their sojourn. And after a couple of days spent in aimless wandering, Shekhar—now looking perturbed and unhappy—came home one evening and told his mother, 'It's getting on my nerves Ma, let's go home.'

Bhuvaneswari at once agreed and said, 'Yes Shekhar, let's go home. It's getting on my nerves, too.'

They returned to Kolkata, arrived home and saw the wall across the roof blocking the passage. Both of them rightly guessed and didn't need to make enquiries—that Nabin did not want any member of his family to speak to Gurucharan, let alone visit them.

When Shekhar was eating his dinner, Bhuvaneswari was present and after a few casual remarks she informed him, 'Lalita is after all getting married to Girin babu. They are negotiating about it. I had guessed it already.'

Without lifting his face Shekhar asked, 'Who told you?'

'It was her mami. I myself went to see them when the karta was having his siesta. She's been crying her eyes out since then.'

Bhuvaneswari fell silent for a moment or two, wiped her eyes with the fringe of her saree and remarked, 'It is fate, Shekhar—fate. No one can reverse what has been allotted—so who do I blame! Be that as it may, Girin is a nice boy—he is affluent too, Lalita will be well taken care of.' And she stopped.

Shekhar said nothing in reply, kept his head down and for a while continued fiddling with his food. After Bhuvaneswari got up and left, he also rose, washed his hands and mouth and went to bed.

The next day when he was out for a little stroll in the evening, the daily tea party was on as usual in Gurucharan's parlour with enough zest, gossip and laughter. The moment the merry noise reached his ears, he paused reflecting for a moment, and then slowly entered the house and following the noise he arrived at

Gurucharan's parlour. At once the babble stopped and as they glanced at his face, the look in their faces changed.

Except Lalita, no one else knew that Shekhar was back home. Today Girindra and another gentleman were present. While the latter continued to stare at Shekhar in amazement, Girindra put on a very solemn expression fixing his gaze on the wall. Gurucharan himself was the most vociferous of them all, now his face absolutely drained of all colour and went white. Seated near him, Lalita was still busy making tea; she glanced up once and then bent her head.

Shekhar drew nearer, bent down and touched the cot with his forehead in a gesture of pranam, sat on the edge, and asked smiling, 'Why—all the lights went out!'

Perhaps Gurucharan pronounced a blessing in a low voice, but it was impossible to follow what he had said.

Shekhar figured out his state of mind and started talking about himself in order to give Gurucharan more time. He jolly well rattled on about their arrival back in the city by a morning train the previous day, his Ma's recovery from illness, news of upcountry and everything else under the sun and at last looked at the strange young man's face.

Gurucharan had by now pulled himself together to some extent. He introduced the young man and said, 'He is a friend of our Girin. They hail from the same place and they went to college together. He's a very good boy. Though he lives in Shyambazar, he often comes by to see me since he made my acquaintance.'

Shekhar shook his head and told himself, 'Yes, certainly a very good boy.' He kept quiet for a little while, then asked, 'Kaka I hope everything is all right?'

Gurucharan said nothing in reply and bowed his head down. The moment Shekhar rose to go, however, he said miserably, 'Do come by sometimes—baba, please don't cut us dead. You've heard everything, haven't you?'

'Of course I have,' said Shekhar and went inside.

Immediately after this, one could hear Gurucharan's wife crying aloud. Gurucharan started wiping his eyes with the tuck of his dhoti and Girin—with a guilty look in his face—looked away out of the window and remained silent. Lalita had already gone inside.

A little later, when Shekhar came out of the kitchen, crossed the veranda and was about to step onto the courtyard, he saw Lalita lurking in the dark behind the door. She knelt and offered pranam to Shekhar, stood up, and nestling against his breast she lifted her face—as if expectantly—silently waiting for a moment or two. Then stepping back, she asked furtively, 'Why didn't you write in reply to my letter?'

'Oh dear, I didn't get any. What did you write?'

'A lot…', said Lalita, and added, 'but leave it alone. You've heard everything. Now tell me—what's your order?'

Amazed, Shekhar exclaimed, 'My order! What good will it do?'

Alarmed, Lalita glanced at his face and asked, 'Why not?'

'So...whom should I order?'

'Me—of course. Whom else can you order?'

'Why should I order you, either? And even if I did, why should you obey?' There was a note of mournful seriousness in Shekhar's voice.

Now Lalita was really frightened, she once more drew close to him and looking as if she was about to cry she said, 'Oh come off it, I'm in no mood for your jokes now. I beseech you, tell me what's going to happen? I'm so afraid I can't sleep at night.'

'Why afraid?'

'Now-really now! How can I not be afraid...when you are not here, Ma isn't here and Mama is up to his antics. What if Ma does not want to accept me as her daughter-in-law?'

Shekhar remained quiet for a moment or two, then he said,'That's right, Ma wouldn't want to. She has heard your Mama borrowed a lot of money from others. Besides, you are now Brahmo and we are Hindu.'

At this point Annakali who was in the kitchen yelled out, 'Sejdi, Ma's calling you.'

Lalita yelled back, 'Coming'. Then, lowering her voice she said, 'No matter whether Mama's Hindu or Brahmo, you are what you are and I am what I am. If Ma can't give you up, she won't give me up, either. As for borrowing money from Girin babu, I'll return it. And a loan must be returned sooner or later.'

Shekhar asked her, 'Where do you think you will get so much money?' Lalita lifted her eyes, fixed her glance on his face, remained silent for a moment and replied, 'Don't you know where women get their money from? I too will get mine the same way.'

Though he had been speaking in a restrained manner till now, Shekhar was smouldering inside and now he mockingly retorted, 'But your Mama has sold you off!'

Lalita could not read the expression in Shekhar's face in the dark, but sensed only too well the alteration in the tone of his voice. She firmly replied, 'That's absolutely untrue. There's no one else like my mama in the world—please don't make fun of him. Perhaps you are not aware of the troubles he's facing and his misery, but the rest of the world knows it.' Having said this she swallowed hard, dithering, and said finally—'besides, he borrowed money after my marriage, hence he has no right to sell me off, nor did he do anything of the sort. Only you have the right. So, if you wish, you can indeed sell me off to avoid shelling out money.' And without waiting for a reply, she quickly strode off.

That night, after wandering about the city streets for hours on end—overwhelmed and shocked, Shekhar returned home pondering: how Lalita, who was just a slip of a girl not so long ago, learnt to talk like this? How could she talk back the way she did in his face like a shameless shrew?

Lalita's behaviour today truly astonished and infuriated him. But if he had calmed down and examined the real cause of his anger, he would have seen that all his anger was directed—not at Lalita—but at himself.

During the last few months spent abroad and away from Lalita, he used to confine himself to his own imaginary world and take stock of only imagined happiness and unhappiness, loss and gain. But as he lay in his bed, his mind repeatedly went over the same ground—the pride of place that Lalita enjoyed in his life, how inextricably linked she was to his future and how terribly hard it was to live without her. Since her childhood Lalita had been a part of their family and precisely because of this he did not consciously imagine her to be just another one of the family like his parents and siblings, nor did it ever occur to him to think along those lines. Perhaps Lalita would not be his, perhaps his parents would not consent to their marriage and she would be someone else's bride. His ominous thoughts repeatedly flowed down this same course and that's why the night before he left Kolkata, he had forcibly garlanded Lalita in a symbolic wedding and thus averted disaster on this side.

While abroad, when the news of Gurucharan's conversion to Brahmo dharma reached him, he was utterly disconsolate and the thought that he might lose Lalita always preyed on his mind. Regardless of its happy or unhappy nature, he was aware of these feelings on only his side. Today Lalita's plain speaking slammed shut this side and drove the current of his thoughts entirely in the opposite direction. Formerly he was concerned lest he lose her, now the problem was how to let go and break off.

Negotiations with the family residing at Shyambazar fell through. They too backed out, baulking at the idea of paying so much money. Shekhar's mother didn't find the girl up to the mark, either. Though Shekhar for the time being had thus got a reprieve from this predicament, Nabin Ray was by no means unmindful of his plans to make money to the tune of ten or twenty thousand rupees from Shekhar's marriage by way of dowry and did not at all remain idle in this regard.

Shekhar wondered what to do. That what he'd done that night would assume such serious proportions, that Lalita would unquestioningly believe that she'd really gotten married to him that night and that it could never be overturned on any account as far as justice was concerned—all this Shekhar had hardly thought through at that time. Although he had himself said these words—what was fated has happened, neither can you reverse it, nor can I—he had neither the ability nor perhaps the leisure to examine the whole business thoroughly as he was doing now.

That night the moon hung overhead, the world was awash with moonlight, he had a garland around his neck, the prospect of having his beloved's heart beat against his for the first time cast a spell on him and there was the very heady desire to drink what lovers have termed the nectar of lips. Self-interest and consideration of worldly loss and gain did not trouble him then, nor did the grim image of his greedy father occur to him. He had reckoned that it wouldn't be so difficult to obtain the consent of his mother who was assuredly fond of Lalita and that if he could get his elder brother to somehow soften their father, the whole thing could perhaps finally fall into place. Besides, at that point in time Gurucharan hadn't withdrawn himself in this way and damned up with rocks the path of their hopes. But now the God of fate himself set his face against them.

Not that Shekhar had much to worry about. Increasingly his conviction grew that it was not possible to persuade even his mother, let alone his father, because now the subject could not be broached to them in any conceivable way.

Shekhar sighed deeply at the thought and once more asked himself almost inaudibly—what to do. He knew Lalita pretty well indeed, he had brought her up with his own hands—she'd by no means give up what she had come to accept as her bounden duty.

She knew that she was no less than Shekhar's lawfully married wife. That is why today in the evening darkness she was capable of doing what she did—she'd unhesitatingly come up to him and drawing close to his breast there she stood—lifting up her face to his.

They've started negotiations for her marriage with Girin, but there is no way they can get her to agree to it. And she'd no longer keep quiet. She'd go and spill her guts all over the place. Shekhar felt hot in the face. Too true. He was not only not content with garlanding each other, he actually went on to hug and kiss her. Lalita didn't resist because she saw nothing wrong in it, because she felt he had a right to do it. Now how could he explain this conduct if he were called to account?

It is granted that they cannot get married without his parents' consent, but how will he show his face once it is known why Lalita cannot marry Girin?

Shekhar had given up all hopes of marrying Lalita because such a marriage appeared impossible to him now. The first few days he was very jittery inside and afraid that she might suddenly turn up and blow the lid off their affair with the result that he would be called to account publicly. But nobody called him to account, it was not clear if the lid had indeed been blown off, nor did anybody from their other house so much as turn up at their place. From the open terrace adjoining his room the entire terrace of Lalita's house could be seen and he altogether stopped going to his terrace lest he should run into her. But a month passed by harmlessly, he sighed with relief and told himself that after all she had a woman's natural instinct for shame and was decisively incapable of naming and shaming him. He had heard that women would rather keep mum than let on even if their hearts were broken. He now believed it and was all praise for the wisdom of the Creator who had saddled women with such a weakness. Yet peace eluded him and he did not know the reason of it. Why was his heart aching in every fibre with a strange, unaccountable pain ever since he concluded that there was no cause for alarm?

And why did disappointment, pain, and fear shake his mind to the core in this manner? And then Lalita would not so much as speak a syllable and remain quiet even when getting married to someone else. Why did he keep smouldering inside whenever he thought that she was now married and gone and busy making her husband's home?

Formerly, instead of going out for a stroll in the evening he used to pace to and fro on the open terrace adjoining his room. Today, too, he was pacing up and down but on none of the days was he able to see anybody of Gurucharan's family come to the terrace. He'd seen only Annakali doing something on the terrace one day, but the moment their eyes met, she averted his gaze and before he could decide whether to call her or not, she'd disappeared. Shekhar could see that even this slip of a girl—Annakali—jolly well understood that they had shut them out by putting up the wall. Another month passed by.

One day Bhubaneswari enquired in course of a conversation, 'Shekhar, have you seen Lalita lately?'

Shekhar shook his head,'No, why?'

Ma went on,'I saw her only yesterday after a couple of months—ran into her on the roof and spoke to her. The poor thing has changed so much—she's grown thinner, her face is drained as if she's grown old. She looks so solemn nobody can say she's only a fourteen-year-old girl.'Tears welled up in Ma's eyes. Wiping the tears with her hands she spoke sadly,'She was wearing a shabby old sari with a hole mended in the fringe of it. I asked her, have run out of saris, dear? She said no. But I don't believe it. You see, she hardly wears anything that her Mama gifts her. Usually I give her saris and dresses. But I didn't buy anything for her in the last six or seven months, either.' She could speak no more. She began wiping her eyes with her sari. Bhubaneswari loved Lalita as if she was her own daughter.

Shekhar sat silently—looking away in another direction. After a pretty long pause she resumed, 'And she can't bring herself to ask anybody for anything except me. Even if she is hungry before meal time, she doesn't tell anyone in the family that she must have something to eat; but she would come to me and hang around and I only need to look at her face to find out about it. And Shekhar, I believe that's what it actually is. She goes about pale and depressed, nobody understands her or cares to ask her anything. It is not that she just calls me Ma, she loves me as she would love her mother.'

Shekhar dared not turn his eyes towards his mother. He kept looking away but said, 'Well Ma, why not call her to find out what she needs and then you can give her whatever it is?'

'Why should she accept anything from Ma? Your father has even blocked the passage connecting the houses. And I can't face seeing her, not to speak of giving her anything. Now it's true that her Mama has done something wrong without realizing it, owing to the pangs of misery. And what have we done? Instead of persuading him to perform *prayaschitta* and thus put it all behind him as his own people would, we have upped and cast him out altogether. I'll also say that he gave up his caste because your father bullied him. He pressed Gurucharan so hard for repaying the loan. Overcome with self-hatred a man can do anything. I'd rather say Gurucharan has done well. That boy Girin—he is like their own kin, much more than we have ever been. Mark my words. After they get married, Girin and Lalita will indeed be a happy couple. I hear they are going to get married next month.'

Turning his face suddenly Shekhar asked, 'Getting married next month?'

'That's what I have heard.'

Shekhar did not ask any more questions.

After a few moments' silence Ma spoke again, 'Lalita tells me her mama isn't keeping well, either. No wonder he is ill. On the one hand she has no peace of mind herself, on the other the whole house is full of moans. No one can have a moment's peace over there.'

Shekhar was listening quietly and he remained quiet.

When Ma left after a little while, he lay down on his bed—started thinking of Lalita.

This lane was so narrow that two carriages could not smoothly move abreast unless one pulled over very close to its side of the lane to let the other pass. About ten days after this, Shekhar's office carriage taking him back home had to stop before Gurucharan's house, the way was blocked by another carriage. Shekhar got off and found out after an enquiry that a doctor had come.

A few days before this he had been told by his mother that Gurucharan wasn't keeping well. Now reminded of this he didn't go home; instead he went straight into Guruharan's bedroom. It was only too true. Gurucharan lay—as if devoid of all strength. Lalita and Girin sat on one side looking worried stiff and the doctor was busy examining his patient.

In a barely audible voice Guru asked him to sit down. Lalita pulled the *anchal* of her sari a little more over her head like a veil and turned her face away.

The doctor lived in the neighbourhood and was familiar with Shekhar. Having examined the condition of the patient's ailment and prescribed medicines he came out taking Shekhar with him and sat outside. Girin followed them to pay his fees. He warned Girin—drawing his attention to the fact that the ailment was as yet in an early stage when a change of air was absolutely necessary.

Once the doctor left, both of them again trooped into Gurucharan's room. Lalita signalled Girin to come away to her and they started talking very quietly, furtively while Shekhar sat silently before Gurucharan staring at him. But Guruharan had already rolled over and was not aware of Shekhar's return.

Shekhar remained seated for a while, then rose and left. Even as he was leaving, Lalita and Girin went on talking furtively. None of them asked him to resume his seat or request him to come again or so much as spoke a word.

Today he came away absolutely convinced that Lalita had forever released him from his stern responsibility. Now he could breathe in, breathe out free from all anxious dread—being certain that Lalita would not ever again involve him in her affairs. As he was changing in his room, he was constantly reminded that today he had seen with his own eyes that it was Girin who had emerged as the greatest friend of that family and the future refuge of Lalita—on whom were pinned all their hopes. On the other hand he was a cipher, counted for nothing and even at this hour of crisis Lalita wasn't looking to him for any assistance or assurance.

Suddenly he exclaimed 'Oh' and flopped onto a cushioned chair bending his head. When he saw her, Lalita had drawn the fringe of her sari as a veil and turned her face away as though he was a total stranger—absolutely unknown and unfamiliar. And right under his eyes she had unending palavers with Girin! And yet Shekhar was the man whose tutelage had once prevented her even from going to the theatre.

Even now he tried to reason with himself that perhaps she had behaved the way she did from a sense of shame because she had their secret relationship at the back of her mind. But how was it possible? If it was so, it was surely very strange that though so much had happened, she never once tried in all these days to ask him anything even through cunning indirect tactics?

Suddenly his mother's voice was heard in the room—she called out, 'Hello! You haven't even washed your hands and face—it's evening.'

Shekhar busily got up and tilting his face to avert her eyes quickly went downstairs.

The past few days many a thought in many a form kept crossing his mind; but there was one question that he would never ponder, namely, who was to blame. So far he had not so much as spoken a word of hope to her or given her a chance to speak a syllable. Rather he was scared stiff lest the secret spilled out in the open, lest she spoke up and advanced her claims. Even so he pinned all the blame on Lalita and held her responsible while at the same time he was being utterly consumed and devastated inside by his own jealousy, fury, pride, and sense of humiliation. Perhaps this is how all men in the world judge and this is exactly how they get burnt out.

He had been smouldering for a week and today in the evening too as he sat in the silent room, the fire he had kept going inside was raging when he heard footfalls near the door, looked up and his heart thumped with excitement. Lalita came in clutching Kali's hand and sat down quietly on the carpet. Kali said,'Shekharda, we have come to offer you our pranam—we are leaving tomorrow.'

Unable to speak, Shekhar looked on.

Kali went on,'We did many silly things in your presence, please try to forget them.'

Shekhar could see at once that every syllable of what Kali was saying she had been tutored to speak, she was merely regurgitating. He asked,'Where are you going?'

'Mungher. We'll take father to Mungher—all of us will go. Girin babu has a house there. Even when he gets better, we won't be able to come back. Doctor says that father won't find this part congenial any more.'

Shekhar enquired,'How is he now?'

'Slightly better,' said Kali. Then producing a few pairs of garments from under the fringe of her sari and showing them to Shekhar, Kali said,'Jethaima has bought us these things.'

Lalita who had been quiet so long, now rose to her feet. She walked up to the table, put a key down on it and explained, 'I have had the key to this cabinet all these days.' She flashed a feeble smile, adding, 'but there's no money left in it, all of it has been spent.'

Shekhar remained silent.

Kali said, 'Let's go Sejdi, it's getting late.'

Before Lalita could get a word in, Shekhar suddenly grew busy and said, 'Kali my dear, please go downstairs and bring me a couple of paans.'

Lalita grasped Kali's hand in her own, pleading, 'You stay here, Kali. I'll go fetch the paan.' And she hurried downstairs. A little later she came back with the paan which she handed over to Kali and the latter gave it to Shekhar.

Shekhar took the paan and sat silently.

'Well Shekharda, we are off,' said Kali. She came up and kneeling down, she offered pranam at Shekhar's feet. Lalita knelt down where she was standing and offered pranam. Then both of them left unhurriedly.

With all his good qualities, all his warts and all his self-dignity intact, Shekhar sat on, his face drained and drawn, silent, stunned. Lalia came and said what she had to say, said goodbye and left never to return, while Shekhar could manage to say nothing. The moments passed as if he had nothing to say. Lalita had deliberately brought Kali along to forestall any undesirable discussion or talk and Shekhar could figure it all out. After this he felt faint and giddy all over. Rising he went and lay down in his bed and closed his eyes.

Even in Mungher's salubrious climate Gurucharan's failing health did not recover. Only a year later he passed away—finally divesting himself of his load of misery. Girin was really very fond of him and did his utmost till he breathed his last. Shortly before his death Gurucharan had grasped Girin's hands and tearfully implored him that he should not ever drift away from his family and that their profound friendship should mature into even closer family ties. He was not destined to see it happen with his own eyes, a variety of illnesses and ailments consumed most of his life, but he wished he would be able to see it all come true from heaven. Gladly and with all his heart Girin had promised to fulfill all his wishes.

Now and then Bhubaneswari had news from abroad of Gurucharan's family relayed to her by the tenants who had rented Gurucharan's house in Kolkata. They also informed her of Gurucharan's death.

Then a disaster struck her own family. Nabin Ray died. Distraught and wild with grief Bhubaneswari placed her elder daughter-in-law in charge of the family and retired to Varanasi saying that she would come back next year after the completion of all the arrangements for Shekhar's marriage and stay only long enough for the marriage to take place before returning to Varanasi.

Nabin Ray had himself finalized the matrimonial match and the marriage would have already taken place had it not been delayed a year by his death. The bride's family was anxious to avoid any more delay and came over to do the ashirvad yesterday. The marriage was slated to take place in the current month. Today Shekhar was preparing to leave for Varanasi in order to bring his mother back home in Kolkata. As he got busy unloading things from the cabinet to put in his suitcase, he was reminded of Lalita after a long time—after all it was Lalita who used to do all these chores.

It was more than three years since they had left and meanwhile he had had no news of them. Nor did he try to find out about them, perhaps because he didn't wish to. Increasingly a hatred for Lalita grew in his mind. But today he was suddenly gripped by the wish. If he could somehow find out how they were getting on. Of course they were supposed to be well off because he knew that Girin was affluent. Yet he wanted to know when they got married, if they were living happily together and so on.

The tenants who had rented Gurucharan's house left a couple of months ago. Shekhar thought he would go and ask Charu's father. Surely he would have news of Girin. Putting off the packing up for a moment or two he stared through the window—a vacant stare—musing over these things. This was when their old housemaid arrived at the door and said, 'Chhotobabu, Kali's mother has sent you word to go and see her.' Turning to face her Shekhar asked, very surprised, 'Which Kali's mother?'

The maid pointed to Gurucharan's house down the lane and explained, 'Our Kali's mother, Chhotobabu. They returned last night.'

'Well, I'm coming,' he said and went down at once.

The day was declining and as soon as he set foot in Gurucharan's house, heartbreaking cries rose in the air. He went up to Gurucharan's wife who was now wearing a widow's garments. Shekhar sat down on the ground, silently wiping the tears from his eyes with the tuck of his dhoti. It was not only his grief for Gurucharan, he was once more overcome with great sadness over his father's death too.

When evening came, Lalita turned up and lit the lamp in the room. She put the fringe of her sari round her neck, made obeisance to him from a distance and after a brief wait she slowly withdrew. Shekhar could not bring himself to look up at or speak to this seventeen-yea-old wife of another man. But from what he could manage to see of her when he glanced askance at her, Lalita seemed to have grown bigger and much thinner than before.

The import of what Gurucharan's widow said after weeping profusely was that she wanted to sell this house and return to and live in Mungher where her son-in-law would look after her. Sehar's father had since long wanted to buy this house. Now if they bought it at a reasonable price, it would be as if the property remained in her own hands. The deal would not inconvenience Shekhar, either, and if she paid a visit here in the future, she too would be able to stay here for a few days and so on. Shekhar assured her that he would consult his mother and do his utmost. Then she wiped her eyes and asked, 'Didi will return in the meanwhile, won't she, Shekhar?'

Shekhar informed her that he was leaving that very night to go and bring her back. Next she subjected Shekhar to a series of questions and received all the pieces of information one after another, such as when the marriage was slated to take place and where, how many thousands of rupees the dowry was worth, the number of ornaments purchased, how Nabin Ray died, what his mother did then and so on. She spoke a lot and heard a great deal.

When Shekhar was at last free, it was dark and the moon was up. Just then Girin came down and went out, most probably to look up his elder sister. Gurucharan's widow then said, 'Shekhar, you don't know my son-in-law, do you? Indeed it is hard to find another boy like him in this world.'

Shekhar said he had no doubt about it and he knew Girin. Then he quickly came away. But on his way out he had to suddenly halt before the parlour.

Lalita was standing by the door in the dark and she asked, 'Listen, are you leaving today itself to go and bring Ma back?'

'Yes.'

'She is very distraught, isn't she?'

'Yes, she was almost mad with grief.'

'And how are you?'

'I'm all right,' said Shekhar and hastened away.

As he hit the road, he shivered with disgust all over. He felt as if even his body had suffered physical desecration because he was obliged to stand close to Lalita. After he returned to his room, he somehow packed his suitcase, closed it and having made sure that the train he would be travelling by would not depart for hours yet, he once more took to bed promising himself to cauterize and burn to cinders the venomous memory of Lalita and now he set off a conflagration of hatred in every pore of his being. The anguish of the burning drove him to mentally subject her to filthy abuse, even call her a slut. In course of their conversation in the evening Gurucharan's widow had said, it was not the kind of marriage made in happiness, that's why they forgot all about it. But Lalita had asked us to inform you all about the marriage. It was this insolence on Lalita's part which especially rankled and seemed to blaze furiously towering over the conflagration already burning away in his mind.

His marriage was still ten or twelve days away when Shekhar returned home with his mother. A couple of days later Lalita was sitting by Bhubaneswari in the morning and loading something on a tray. Shekhar didn't know that Lalita was there, so he came in calling 'Ma' on some errand or the other and was at once taken aback. Lalita got on with her work and kept her head down.

Ma asked, 'What is it baba?'

Having quite forgotten what he had come to see her about, he said, 'Oh, it's nothing, I'll do it later,' and hurried off. He could not see Lalita's face but her hands did not escape his notice and he saw that she was wearing no ornament except a pair of glass bangles on each wrist. Shekhar sniggered and told himself that she was putting on a kind of innocent act. He knew that Girin was affluent. He saw no reason why his wife should be wearing no gold ornaments such as bangles or bracelets.

That morning he was quickly coming down the stairs and Lalita too was ascending the same stairs and she stood aside to let him pass. But as soon as Shekhar came alongside, she said very hesitantly and quietly, 'There is something I would like to tell you.'

For a moment Shekhar stood still and rather astonished he wondered, 'Who? Me?'

Lalita replied quietly as before, 'Yes, you.'

'What on earth is there to tell me!' He said and rushed down the stairs even more swiftly than before.

Lalita stood stock-still for a few moments, then she sighed and slowly went away.

The next morning Shekhar was poring over the day's newspaper in their parlour when looking up he was very astonished to see Girin come in. Girin offered namaskar and greeted him and pulling a chair sat close by. Shekhar returned his namaskar and waited with a questioning look in his face. Though they had a nodding acquaintance, they were none too familiar with each other and neither of them had so long displayed any keenness to increase mutual familiarity.

Girin straightaway came to the point. He explained, 'A pressing necessity compels me to obtrude on you. You have of course heard what my mother-in-law intends to do, she wants to sell the house to you. Today she sends word through me that she can return to Munghер this month itself if an arrangement of some kind can soon be worked out in this regard.'

From the moment he saw Girin arrive, a storm was raging in Shekhar's heart. He didn't at all take kindly to what Girin was saying and looking rather sullen, he replied, 'That's quite right.

But after father's death my dada is now the owner of everything. It will be naturally necessary to consult him.'

Smiling quietly, Girin said,'We also know that. But it will be better if you speak to him.'

Shekhar replied in the same fashion,'It will also serve the purpose if you speak. Now you are the guardian on the other side.'

Girin said, 'Of course I can if I have to. But yesterday Sejdi was saying that the matter could be easily settled if you gave it a little attention.'

So long Shekhar was reclining on the plump cushion as he talked, but now he sat up bolt upright and asked, 'Who did you was saying it?'

Girin clarified,'Sejdi—I mean Lalitadi was saying...'

Shekhar was utterly stupefied with astonishment. Not a syllable of what Girin was saying entered his ears. He stared at Girin's face with dazed eyes and then said,'You will excuse me Girin babu, but you got married to Lalita, did you not?'

Considerably embarrassed, Girin stuck out and bit his tongue in dismay and explained,'No...not really...you know all of them of course...I married Kali.'

'But that's not what was originally decided upon.'

Girin who had heard everything from Lalita said,'That is right, it's not what was originally decided upon. Before he died, Gurucharan babu had implored me not to marry outside his family. For my part, I also promised to abide by his wish. After his death Sejdi explained to me—though nobody else knows anything about it—that she was already married and her husband was alive. Perhaps nobody else would have credited it, but I believed every word of what she told me. Besides, a woman can marry only once—hello- what's wrong?'

Shekhar's eyes were already swimming with tears and now the tears streamed down from the corners of his eyes even in front of Girin. But Shekhar was hardly aware of it, nor did he at all remember that it was very disgraceful for a man to betray such weakness before another man.

Girin sat gazing silently. Certainly he had his own hunch and today he knew for certain who was Lalita's husband. Shekhar wiped his eyes and asked in a voice thick with emotion, 'But you have great affection for Lalita, don't you?'

Girin's face darkened with deep-seated distress, but the very next moment he was smiling quietly. Unhurriedly he explained, 'That is not very important or pertinent. Besides, no matter how strong one's affection is, one does not knowingly go and marry another man's wife. Anyway, I don't want to talk about these things where our elders are concerned.' Flashing another smile he stood up and concluded, 'Well, I'm off. I will see you later.' He offered Shekhar his namaskar and exited.

All along Girin had been the object of Shekhar's envy and of late this envy had grown into a profound hatred. But today, no sooner had Girin left than Shekhar rose to his feet and coming up lay himself down on the ground and touched the ground repeatedly with his forehead—thus offering pranams to this all but unknown Brahmo young man. For the first time in his life he now saw how a man could noiselessly perform monumental self-sacrifice and smilingly keep a severe grim vow.

When he went into his mother's room and sat on her bed in the afternoon, Bhubaneswari was sitting on the floor and aided by Lalita she was carefully piling up heaps of new clothing in neatly arranged stacks. Today he did not run away at the sight of Lalita. Glancing up Ma said, 'What's the matter dear?' Shekhar remained silent and watched how the stacks were shaping up. A little later he enquired, 'What are you doing Ma?' Ma replied, 'I am adding up to see how many new garments I will need to give as gifts to people. I guess we will have to buy some more—am I right dear?'

Lalita nodded in agreement.

Smiling Shekhar quizzed her, 'And what if I don't marry Ma?'

Bhubaneswari also smiled and replied, 'You're perfectly capable of doing that. I wouldn't put anything past you.'

Shekhar smiled again and said, 'Perhaps that's what it is coming to, Ma.'

Ma grew serious and protested, 'What a thing to say! Don't let such inauspicious things even pass your lips.'

Shekhar replied, 'Till now I haven't, but I can't help it now. If I remain silent, I am afraid a terrible wrong will take place.'

Very much at sea, Bhubaneswari looked on in consternation. Shekhar went on, 'You have in the past forgiven many a folly committed by this son of yours. Please forgive this one too, Ma. I can't really marry the girl you have chosen.'

What her son said and the expression in his face truly alarmed her, but in a bid to conceal her feelings Bhubaneswari gushed, 'Well, well, I will let you have your way. Now please leave me alone Shekhar, don't badger me. I have so many things to do.'

Once more Shekhar tried in vain to smile and admitted in a dry tone, 'Yes Ma, I am telling you the truth. This marriage cannot take place.'

'Why ever not? Is it child's play?'

'Exactly, Ma. I am saying all this because it's not child's play.'

Now really frightened and perturbed, Bhubaneswari retorted angrily, 'Now Shekhar come on, make a clean breast of what is going on. I don't like all this dodgy talk.'

Shekhar said quietly, 'I will tell you some other day Ma…some other day.'

'You will tell me some other day!' She thrust aside the stack of clothes and exclaimed, 'Make arrangements so that I can go to Varanasi this very day. I don't want to spend even a single night with such a family.'

Shekhar sat keeping his head down.

Growing even more agitated she said, 'Lalita also wants to go to Varanasi with me. Let us see if I can't fix her up with something.'

Now Shekhar lifted his face and said smiling, 'You will take her to Varanasi with you. Who else is there to decide on this? Yours is the last word as far as she is concerned.'

It was as if seeing his smiling face made her somewhat more hopeful than before and glancing at Lalita she exclaimed, 'Hear him talk dear! He thinks I can take you anywhere I want to. We must have her aunt's permission, mustn't we?'

Lalita did not say anything. The way Shekhar was talking enormously embarrassed her.

Shekhar blurted out, 'If you want to let her know, do it by all means—if that's what you want. But whatever you wish will be done. This is what I believe and so does she whom you want to take along. She is your daughter-in-law.' Shekhar said and bent his head.

Bhubaneswari was petrified with amazement. Was this the kind of jest he would make to her face! Fixing him with her gaze she demanded, 'What did you say? What did you say she is to me?'

Shekhar could not bring himself to lift his face, but managed to reply all the same. Slowly he enunciated, 'I have already said it, Ma. Not that it has happened just today, it has been like this for more than four years. You have really and truly been a mother to her. I can't say any more, Ma. Ask her and she will tell you all.' As he finished his sentence, he could see that Lalita had put the anchal of her sari round her neck in the traditional way to offer pranam to Ma. He too rose, went and stood by her side. Then both of them bent down to offer pranam and touch her feet. The next moment Shekhar left quietly.

Bhubaneswari was now shedding tears of joy. She had indeed an immense affection for Lalita. Opening her chest she brought out all her jewellery and as she made Lalita put on each and every piece, she learnt from her everything bit by bit. Having heard the whole story she now asked, 'So that's the reason Girin married Kali?'

Lalita replied, 'Yes Ma, that's the reason. I do not know if there are other souls like Girin babu in the world. As soon as I explained everything to him, he believed that I was really a married woman. My husband may or may not accept me, that depends on his will, but he exists.'

Bhubaneswari placed her hand on her head to bless her and exclaimed, 'Of course he is there! And I am blessing him, may he live long life after life. Please sit down and wait a little while I go and tell Abinash that the bride for the wedding has changed.' Saying so she went off smiling in the direction of her elder son's room.

Glossary of Bengali Terms

aapni: as in 'aap' in Hindi to address someone formally.

anchal: the border or edge of a sari used to cover the bodice.

ashirvad: engagement. Prior to the wedding, the bride is formally blessed and presented with jewellery by the bridegroom's parents.

baba: father, dad. Also a term of endearment used by older persons to address male children and younger males generally (corresponding term for females is Ma).

bada-bouma: the elder daughter-in-law—wife of Abinash—the elder son of Nabin and Bhubaneswari.

bhaya: a more familiar, informal form of Bhai (brother).

bouthan: In conversation with Gurucharan, Nabin Ray refers to his wife Bhubaneswari thus.

Brahmo: a religious reform movement in Hindu society initiated by Raja Rammohan Roy.

didi: an elder sister or cousin; also a mode of address.

karta: Bhubaneswari here refers to her husband Nabin Ray thus. A piece of colloquialism.

Jethaima: elder aunt and here refers to Bhubaneswari.

lagna: an auspicious time or moment to perform a religious or social ceremony such as marriage.

ma-janani: a reverential mode of addressing a mother or a motherly woman or a woman benefactor.

Mama: a maternal uncle and a mode of address.

Mami: Mama's wife, maternal aunt.

panjika: Hindu astronomical calendar.

prayaschitta: purificatory rites laid down in the scriptures to be performed in atonement for and expiation of sinful acts. According to orthodox Hindus like Nabin Ray, Gurucharan should perform prayaschitta to atone for the sin of having converted to the Bramho religion which opposed idol worship and the rigidities of the caste system—thus falling foul of the orthodox Hindus. Bramho families often faced hostility and ostracism from such Hindus.

punnya: spiritual merit believed to result from the good actions of a living person, accrue to and benefit the person in the next rebirth.

sai: pal, friend. Used as a mode of address by girls and young women (old-fashioned).

sai-ma: an affectionate and respectful mode of address formerly used by youngsters while speaking to a motherly woman.

Shaktishela: the powerful weapon shot by Ravana to knock out Lakshmana as narrated in the Ramayana.

Shyambazar: The traditional old northern district of Kolkata.

tattwa: assorted gifts—chiefly sweets and garments—sent to matrimonial relations (groom's parents).

tumi: as in 'tum' (you) in Hindi to address someone informally.

Subhransu Maitra (born 1952) was educated at Presidency College, Kolkata and Banaras Hindu University. He is now Superintendent, Publication at Netaji Subhas Open University, Kolkata. A distinguished translator, he translates modern Bengali literature into English.

Maitra's published translations include Sankha Ghosh's *The Gaandharbha Cycle of Poems* (2003), an anthology of Mahasweta Devi's short stories—*Wrong Number and Other Stories* (2005), an anthology of Jibanananda Das's poems—*Jibanananda* (2007), an anthology of Bengali short stories written by women—*Here and Beyond* (2007), a critical study of Jibanananda Das—*Endless Night and Eternal Sunrise* (with Sumita Chakrabarti, 2009), *Letters of Rabindranath Tagore* (Vol. 1, 2012) and a collection of Tagore's thoughts on education—*Education as Freedom: Tagore's Paradigm* (Niyogi Books, 2014).